Having a Ball and Other Stories

Lynn Otty

To Maureen
Reading will
keep us young,
right?
Lynn

ISBN: 197810801X
ISBN-13: 978-1978108011

DEDICATION

For
my family.

"Lynn Otty is a natural storyteller. While her themes are wide-ranging and diverse, she maintains an acute attention to detail which leaves us with images and vignettes which linger long after reading is complete. We meet cowboy heroes, kamikaze pilots, misguided and misbehaving children and an assortment of unfortunate characters in unsettling situations. Whether it's a night journey in a foreign land, a child by a corpse in a funeral parlour, a cleaning team in an unsavoury house, this writer does not shy clear of society's shadier places.

This is a long awaited but most welcome collection."

Liz Niven, author of *The Shard Box*

"This is a compelling collection of short stories and micro fiction. Lynn Otty possesses the knack of effortlessly drawing the reader into each of these narratives. I was impressed with their variety and range. She demonstrates too an ability to assume different viewpoints with facility and conviction and to create settings with deftness and precision. The stories are by turns humorous, poignant and chilling and frequently trip the reader up with denouements that are daring and sometimes shocking. Lynn Otty shows in this her debut as a writer of fiction (she is already a well-established poet) that she has mastered the short story form."

David Mark Williams, author of *The Odd Sock Exchange*

"Lynn Otty's stories range widely from a prairie childhood to the ills of modern day life, by way of a kamikaze pilot, the assassination of Lincoln and more. They are told with economy and imagination and often take us in some unexpected directions, by a writer with an unblinking eye and clearly no fear of the dark."

Sally Hinchcliffe, author of *Out of a Clear Sky*

CONTENTS

COWBOY DAYS

It was the kind of day when everything seems to move in slow motion and the tar along the edge of the road starts running. My brother was out at the front of the house frying eggs on the sidewalk. I was sprawled on a beach towel in the backyard playing with Louie. Dad had set up the sprinkler on the lawn after lunch and I'd spent the last half hour running back and forth through the cold spray. So, I was waiting for my bathing suit to dry and Louie, well, he was just being an ordinary chameleon.

I heard Dorothy's sand shoes clomping along the sidewalk before I even saw her. She plonked herself down on the edge of the stoop to get her breath back before she spoke.

"Kenny, down at the store just told me somethin'. Guess who's coming to town?"

"I dunno." I shrugged. "But I bet you just finished an orange Popsicle."

Dorothy blushed and rubbed her lips hard to destroy the evidence.

"Lash LaRue! He'll be at the Bowladrome on Friday night!"

"What?"

I sat up so quickly my head felt spinny. I grabbed Louie and shoved him into his cage before his claws could latch onto my fingers. Lash LaRue was coming here. In two days. This had to be the most exciting thing to happen in my life, at least since last spring when my cat Charlie turned into Charlene and had six kittens in my clothes closet.

I leapt up and jumped over the sprinkler a couple of times just to cool my excited brain. Dorothy grabbed my hand in the spirit of the moment and joined me, even though she had shorts on. Lash LaRue had to be my all-time favourite cowboy. I read stories about him week after week in the comic books down at the drugstore. Sometimes my brother and I even bought them.

I mean, I liked all the cowboys – Roy Rodgers, Gene Autrey, Red Ryder - but Lash LaRue? - I *loved* him. In fact, I sometimes dreamt that when I grew up I would go to his ranch and he'd fall madly in love with me and we'd get married and live happily ever after.

But that was my secret.

Trailing water, we raced through the kitchen and up the stairs to my bedroom. I slammed the door; belly-flopped onto the bed and stretched my arm underneath to pull out the box of comics. We sat cross-legged on the floor searching the dog-eared contents for any that featured our hero. When we found them we stared in silent adoration at the pages. Oh, that handsome face, that square jaw. The way he handled that bullwhip.

"Look at his outfit," Dorothy said.

"And his horse."

I shook my head with the wonder of it all.

"Isn't it enough to make you swoon?"

It was. And we did.

We lolled away the rest of the afternoon discussing all the exciting possibilities that could come about as a result of meeting our hero in the flesh. The best thing would be that Lash would see us in the audience and decide on the spot that he couldn't work without Dorothy and me as his faithful assistants from that moment on.

All night in dreams I galloped across the grassy plain rounding up thundering herds of mighty mustangs; manes flying, hooves pounding. Handsome, rugged cowboys, each with the face of Lash LaRue, rode alongside me.

After breakfast I made up a package of grape Freshie and poured it over some ice cubes into the canteen. Then I made enough peanut butter and jam sandwiches to feed a whole Brownie troupe. Just in case. I hopped on my bike and raced round to the Esso corner where I'd agreed to meet Dorothy. We'd decided if we didn't do something to keep ourselves occupied, Friday would seem like it was never going to get here. It was a perfect time to cycle out to Picklepuss and hunt for Indian arrowheads around the lake. That was about seven miles out in the country so it would be an all-day expedition.

The ruts in the track that led to the lake from the main road were deep and baked hard as concrete by the prairie sun. We sped downhill toward a bunch of stunted birch trees and Dorothy flew past me. Her hair was streaming out behind her and she was whooping like a wild Indian. As she leaned forward her front wheel caught in one of the ruts. I stood up on my pedals and picked up speed.

"Slow down, Dorothy – stop pedalling!"

In what seemed like slow motion, I watched her lose control and sail right over the handlebars and out of sight. It happened in the blink of an eye. When I caught up and jumped off my bike, all I could see were her feet sticking out of the tall grass in the ditch.

"Dorothy, Dorothy - you alright? You haven't broken anything, have you?"

There was a muffled reply and her head slowly appeared above the foxtails. She was pale and her lips clamped together as she got up. Pulling leaves from her hair with one hand and wiping her face with the other, she limped over to inspect her bike.

"You kids okay?"

We nearly jumped out of our skins as we turned and squinted into the sun. A horse was standing behind us on the other side of the track. In the saddle was a man wearing jeans and a black cowboy shirt with a red bandana around his neck. The face under the Stetson smiled.

"Anybody hurt here?" He looked from us to our abandoned bikes. We both shook our heads and continued staring at him.

"Hey," he said as he dismounted, "what's the matter? Cat got yer tongue?"

He dropped the reins and walked towards us.

It was then I noticed the horse. It looked just like Buckskin.

Buckskin? My jaw fell open.

"Is that…? Are you…?"

I couldn't bring myself to ask. It was like being in a waking dream. Dorothy looked at my face and then jerked her eyes back to the cowboy.

"…Lash LaRue?"

"Now how did you know that?"

"You're coming to town tomorrow." I said. My heart was beating as though I'd just run a race.

"We're going to see you."

"Glad to hear it." He winked and moseyed over to Dorothy's bike, picked it up and readjusted the handlebars.

"What are you doing out here? At Picklepuss?"

"Well, ol' Buckskin and me, we get kinda lonesome now and then for the wide open plains, don't we boy?" The horse swayed as if he knew what the cowboy was saying. He nodded his massive head and whinnied softly.

"So when we've got a couple of days between shows we scout out a spot where we can set up camp and take it easy for awhile. If you look over there you can just see our trailer by those bushes."

Sure enough, there it was. It was small and dusty and it looked like it had travelled lots of miles, but it was Lash LaRue's alright. It had his name painted along the side in flashy black and gold writing.

He squatted down beside us.

"What are you little buckaroos doing out here? You're pretty far from town."

"Aw, we come out here all the time to look for arrowheads."

"And maybe today we'll even find a broken arrow!" Dorothy said.

"Sounds like fun. Mind if an old cowboy tags along?"

Lash seemed as happy with our company as we were with his. Once we got used to the idea, being with him wasn't much different than being with Ralph, Dad's hired man. I've noticed before that sometimes grownups can act just like little kids when there aren't any other grownups around to see them.

We spent quite a long time looking for arrowheads around the lake but ended up finding a few sparrows' nests and a small snake instead.

"Watch out, girls!"

Before either of us had time to take a breath, Lash grabbed his hunting knife from its holder on his belt, threw it at the snake and pinned the poor thing to the ground in front of our very eyes. Dorothy and I stood in stunned silence and watched, fascinated, as it squirmed and writhed in its death throes. We knew it was only a garter snake and couldn't hurt anybody.

"Why did you kill it, Lash?" I was swallowing hard.

"Well, I didn't want to have to treat either of you for snakebite."

He retrieved his knife and wiped the guck off the blade down the leg of his jeans before returning it to its sheath.

Lash poked at the tiny body with the toe of his boot to be sure it was truly dead and then he picked it up and swung it around over his head like a lasso. He showed us how to skin it by slitting the belly from under its jaw right down to the tip of its tail and carefully separating the skin from the innards. It came off in one piece and it was fine and beautiful. Green and gold and black. He stretched it around the crown of his hat and said that once it dried in that position, it would probably stay there forever. And it would always remind him of us. He said he might just cook the snake on his campfire that night and eat it for his supper, but we didn't believe him.

A woman's voice called from the trailer.

"Gerry-y-y…"

"Gerry, baby…"

Lash kept smiling as he turned toward the trailer. But I knew he was mad because his eyes closed to slits the way my dad's sort of do just before he gives me serious heck.

"I told you to make yourself scarce."

The screen door opened and a young woman walked out. Her feet were bare and her shirt was hanging outside her jeans. I thought I'd recognised the voice.

"Is that Diane Cooper?"

It sure was and I wondered what she was doing in Lash's trailer. She was a teenager who hung around the café even on school nights playing the pinball machine and smoking cigarettes, with her hair in pin curls. I even saw her sitting in a booth drinking coffee with some travelling salesmen. Mom said she was wild.

"You know her?" Lash seemed surprised.

"Yeah – what's she doin' here?"

"Well, she's…my, uh… cousin."

"That's right." Diane sashayed up behind Lash and shoved both her hands deep into his back pockets.

"I'm his kissin' cousin."

Smiling, she stared straight at Dorothy and I and then she did something very rude – she snuggled into him and whispered something in his ear right in front of us. Everybody knows you are not supposed to whisper. Lash just grinned as he listened and raised one eyebrow. Then he patted her bottom and gave her a little push toward the trailer. She knew we were all watching her as she sauntered back.

"Why did she call you Gerry?"

"That's her pet name for me."

"But listen, girls," He leaned over and put his arms around our shoulders, "this will be our secret, right?"

We nodded.

"Promise?"

We nodded again.

I looked at Dorothy and she looked at me. We both grinned at the thought of sharing a secret with Lash LaRue. If he had asked us to, I know we would have sworn it in our own blood.

Instead he told us that to make up for the fact that we didn't find any arrowheads, and as a treat for keeping our secret, he would put on a private show just for us. We thought that would be fantastic. He called Diane to come out and join us. The three of us girls sat in the shade and shared the sandwiches I had brought along. Dorothy and I took turns drinking the Freshie out of the canteen while Diane drank beer. She even asked if we wanted a sip from her bottle. We felt excited and very grownup. We decided she was quite nice really.

Lash performed all sorts of stunts with Buckskin. First they galloped around in circles that got smaller and smaller and smaller until Buckskin was twirling on the spot. Then Lash jumped to the ground and got Buckskin to canter by himself in a larger circle. The second time around he took a running jump, grabbed a handful of Buckskin's mane and leapt right into the saddle in one go. While they were still moving he turned and sat backwards and then forwards again.

Next he stood beside Buckskin.

"Hey boy, what's two and two?"

The horse pawed the ground four times. I didn't know a horse could be that smart. And when we clapped Buckskin bent down on one leg and took a bow. Lash grabbed his bull whip off the saddle horn.

"Diane, stand up. Hold your beer bottle out with a

straight arm and whatever you do, don't move."

Quick as a flash he flicked the whip and it went right around the neck of the bottle. Diane let out a little scream while Dorothy and I cheered and clapped until our hands were sore.

But the best trick of all was when he laid down on the ground and Buckskin lay on top of him. I was a bit scared but when Buckskin got back up, so did Lash. He brushed the dust off his jeans and wasn't hurt at all.

Later he let us each have a little ride alone on Buckskin and I thought heaven couldn't be better than this. All the while I was on Buckskin's back I crooned into his velvety ears.

"I love you, Buckskin. I love you, boy."

And I know he was listening to me.

When the show was over we set out for home. As we pedalled away we heard Diane's voice calling after us.

"Hey! see you later, alligator."

We looked back and whooped,

"After a while, crocodile."

Having a Ball and Other Stories

HEADING HOME

"'Where are we going, exactly?'" She turned her head and peered through the grimy window at the lacquered black of the sky, while ancient gears protested as the car stuttered left onto the autobahn. There were no stars to be seen. The road was empty except for an occasional vehicle speeding by. The man in the back seat leaned forward. His head was uncomfortably close to hers. She could smell his aftershave as he and the driver spoke in quiet tones almost as though they were alone. She put her hand into the pocket of her coat and felt around for her mobile phone. It wasn't there. She must have stashed it in her handbag when she was on the train.

"Apparently we go to a village about ten minutes from the airport."

That didn't tell her anything. Didn't the village have a name? She began to wonder at her own naivety. She couldn't believe that she was sitting in a strange beat-up old car, hurtling through the darkness with no idea of where she was being taken. This really didn't compute with her role as line manager within the corporation back in London. There would be a few raised eyebrows amongst members of her team in the HR department if they ever got wind of this venture. And yet right now none of her friends, family or workmates knew where she was.

What if this whole thing was a set-up? They had appeared late at night at the reservation counter in the airport - the young, handsome man who could conveniently speak her language, lulling her into a false sense of security; the old grandfatherly type who could be pretending not to understand anything she said so that they could talk and make plans without her, their victim, understanding a word. The more she considered her situation, the more uneasy she became. This could be some sort of kidnap ring - or worse.

She had read about people who simply disappeared in foreign countries. She'd always wondered how they could get themselves into such dangerous situations without even realising it. Yet here she was, doing the same sort of thing. That girl at the desk? Hadn't she practically pushed her into their arms? Maybe she was in cahoots with them. Maybe they were all part of a gang. She shifted in her seat and reached to the floor for her handbag, trying to stop her thoughts from going any further in that direction.

When she had arrived at the airport, less than an hour ago, it was quieter than she'd expected considering all the disruption to public transport caused by the fierce overnight storm. It was late. Her flight home had departed long ago. She was tired, ravenous, and she had a banger of a headache. The right wheel on her suitcase had jammed as it rolled over a small piece of paper on the polished granite floor. She'd frowned, given it a fierce yank and carried on dragging it towards the information desk.

There was one person standing ahead of her. She turned to the Russian student who walked beside her. Companions for the last ten or so hours, they had been grateful for each other's company in the crowded carriage as their train crawled from town to town during their shared mystery tour. Especially so when they had finally disembarked miles from their ultimate destination in a vast station on the far side of the city. Neither of them had expected the diversion and so had both put on a show of bravado, encouraging each other with smiles and shrugs, as they trolled from platform to platform searching for the line that would hopefully deliver them to the airport. During the last leg of the journey they had chatted almost non-stop, determined to keep one another awake so they wouldn't miss their station. When the student discovered she had minutes only to get to the gate of a later flight to Moscow, they hugged each other and said good-bye as though they were old friends. She watched the girl run toward passport control, then turn around and wave one final time before disappearing into the departure area. She knew their paths were unlikely to cross again.

It was close to midnight. She noticed most of the fast food places around the concourse were closed. Her first priority was to get a bed for what was left of the night; then she would go on a hunt for something to eat.

"How can I help?" Perfect English.

She relaxed a little and stepped up to the desk to explain her predicament to the efficient looking person who had spoken. The woman was sympathetic and told her that there had been many problems on a huge scale all day with delays and missed flights. In fact, quite a number of planes had been grounded for take-off throughout the day. It would be best, she was told, to return to the airport in the morning and arrange another flight when the airline office opened again at nine o'clock.

She thanked the woman and proceeded to plod over to the hotel reservation counter where a younger girl, appearing ridiculously fresh and bright at this late hour, put down the phone and, with a sigh, glanced up at her.

"Is it a single room you are wanting?"

"Yes, please."

At this point she was past caring about the cost. And she certainly wasn't prepared to spend precious time going back into the city by taxi or any other means. If accommodation nearby was expensive, so what? This was the very reason people bought travel insurance.

"Go with him." The girl pointed toward the rope barrier.

A man with grey-brown curly hair that looked as though it could be a wig was standing by himself a few feet away. His large hands dangled down at his sides. He was wearing a dark shiny nylon puff jacket and his mouth was attempting a twisted, toothy grin as he stared through lenses that made his eyes look too large for his pasty face. He reminded her of a well-known plasticine cartoon character back home named Wallace.

"What do you mean – go with him?" She turned back to the counter. "Who is he?"

"He has two single rooms left at his place tonight – forty-five euros. Go with him."

"But is this legitimate? I mean…"

"Yes, yes. You want a room. Just go with him." Having dealt with the query, she flicked the air dismissively with her pink manicured fingernails and turned away to answer the telephone once more.

She noticed a young man who appeared to have overheard her conversation. He was now negotiating with the stocky man to take one of the rooms on offer. He was dressed in slim jeans and a waistcoat and carrying a light-looking duffle bag. He was speaking German without any apparent hesitation. As she approached he turned and greeted her in English. How did they always know, these Continentals? she wondered. He informed her that their host spoke only German and quickly took on the role of interpreter once he had established that she spoke only English. She asked if there would be a café open at the hotel. Or, failing that, room service. The answer was no.

'But I must have something to eat. I've only had one bottle of water since seven-thirty this morning, I've got a terrible headache and I've been stuck on a train going nowhere all day.' She realised she was sounding like a disgruntled child.

The other traveller, who it transpired, was Dutch, translated and returned with the offer of a detour to an all-night drive-through hamburger joint on the way to their accommodation. The thought of all that grease made her feel queasy.

"It's okay. I couldn't face it. Thanks anyway." She desperately needed to sleep.

Outside the airport the cold air felt good on her face. It cleared her head a little as they walked toward the parking area. It reminded her of the fresh mountain air that she had enjoyed so much for the past week and which she had left only that morning, or rather yesterday morning. Any benefits she had gained from her break seemed to be fast disappearing. She was a bit disconcerted as they approached a battered, rusting vehicle and realised this was to be their transport. The Dutchman laughed as the owner opened a back door and began to shove the clutter onto the far side of the seat to make room for one of them.

"I think neither of us has ever had a shuttle like this, eh?" he murmured as he insisted she take the front seat. She could smell the stale odour of the interior from where she was standing. Not very pleasant. Unwashed with traces of garlic, she guessed, as she handed over her case and then settled in next to the driver.

Her anxiety levels soared as the car turned off the road into a darkened lane and slowed right down to a crawl. It pulled up at the side of a square two-story building and the car engine was turned off. It didn't look anything like a hotel to her. She refused the older man's offer to carry her case. She wasn't letting it out of her grasp. He rushed ahead, puffing over the path and up a few stairs. Rattling a huge bundle of keys he unlocked the door. She wondered what would await her inside. She quelled her anxiety with an effort, arguing with herself that she must be safe. Surely nothing bad could happen. This is *me,* not some newspaper article. She followed the man through the entrance and into a short corridor. He closed and locked the outer door then he disappeared behind one of the other doors, pulling it closed after him. She waited beside the Dutchman.

"Please don't go anywhere before you help me sort out my plans to return to the airport in the morning, will you?" She hated the Dutchman seeing that she was feeling so insecure.

"All right." He was picking up his suitcase and starting for the stairs.

"I'm leaving at seven – when do you want to be there?"

"Nine," she said as their host returned with a receipt and asked for his money. He wanted cash.

"This says fifty-nine euros – the girl told me it was only forty-five." She wondered if this was the beginning of... of what?

Another short discussion in German ensued. The Dutchman smiled.

"He says that price includes the shuttle here and back again. Beats sleeping on a chair in the airport, right?"

"Right." She handed over the cash. "Thanks for your help."

So, she had paid in advance for the return trip to the airport. That, in itself, was reassuring.

The old man crossed the hall, opened a door and turned the lights on in her room. As he gave her the keys he gestured that she lock the door behind him. She nodded and did just that. She looked around.

She felt a surge of relief when she saw the room was simply but adequately furnished. Further investigation revealed a small bathroom which was spotlessly clean. On the windowsill above the toilet she discovered a fresh bar of soap sitting on top of a stack of fluffy white towels. She took her coat off and reached for a hanger in the closet. It was very quiet.

There was a knock at the door. She jumped and jerked her head towards the sound. Why was he back? What did he want?

"Just a moment." She took a deep breath and

turned the lock. Standing with her foot against the inside of the door she peered out.

In the corridor the old man stood smiling his odd, toothy smile. He was holding a tray on which there was a loaf of dark bread, a package of sliced salami, a small tub of yoghurt and a bottle of flavoured water. There was a plate with a knife, a spoon and even a napkin. He pushed the offering toward her with an encouraging tilt of his head.

"Bitte. Bitte" His eyes were soft and concerned behind the thick lenses of his glasses. How could she ever have imagined him having evil intentions!

"Oh, Dank, mein Herr." She suddenly recalled another phrase from her guide book and added "Vielen, vielen Dank!"

A slight look of amusement passed over the old man's face. 'Gruss Gott,' he whispered back passing the tray over the threshold. His hands dropped to his sides as he executed a slight old-fashioned bow and turned away. Smiling, she watched him disappear across the hall. Then she closed her door and settled down to savour the unexpected feast before finally curling up between the clean crisp sheets.

Hardly able now to keep her eyes from closing, she dug around in her handbag to find her phone. Although it was late, she thought she would send a quick voicemail to Sarah, her flatmate, saying all was well and she'd regal her about the trip tomorrow night over dinner.

"Damn! No reception."

She put the phone on the table and resolved to get in touch once she got to the airport in the morning. Now it was all she could do to reach over and turn out the lamp.

She didn't hear the light footsteps that came down the stairs and stopped outside her door or notice the shaded headlights of the car that was slowly crawling up the drive.

Having a Ball and Other Stories

A LESSON IN ETIQUETTE

Esther Boulin! How many times have ah tol' you that that is no way fo' a young lady to get out of a caw? Honestly, if yore sweet daddy, brother Ethan or even James Ridley – yes, James Ridley, don't think Ah haven't noticed him makin' calf eyes at you - well, if any of those aforementioned gentlemen opens the do' for you when you have reached you' travel destination you must remember jus' what to do in the circumstances, so listen to yore momma now.

The furs thing t'do is to check that yo' skirt isn't bunched up in a mess, Esther. A'ways give it a quick straighten with yore han' while the driver scoots roun' to yore side of the caw - an' be sure to see that yo' crinoline is tucked b'tween yo' legs b'for you proceed. Yo' knees must a'ways be togetha, darlin', like they are clamped, as in one graceful movement you swing yo' legs out of the caw and place yo' feet daintily 'pon the ground. Toes furs, a' course. Next, you lean yo' upper torso fo'ward whilst reachin' out fo' the armrest on the door with one hand and extendin' yo' free hand for yo' escort to clasp as he offers his assistance – don't grab, Esther, never grab – jus' lay yore hand 'pon his – palm to palm. All gentlemen find this light physical contact fairly makes their heart race, yore dear daddy has sworn to me.

As you alight from the caw with yore hand restin' in his, jus' take a moment to observe whetha the seams in yore stockin's are straight because crooked seams are definitely the sign of a person who not only has little regard fo' herself but also none for those in her company. Remember that, ma little sugarplum. It's a verra important point. Straight seams go a long way in what they say about a lady.

Now don't go lookin' away from me, missy, when Ah'm engaged in impartin' instruction to you of what is considered acceptable etiquette fo' a young lady standin' 'pon the cusp of womanhood. It is up to you neva to fo'get that you are a Boulin - that the Boulin name is the most respected name in these parts - and therefo' our family must a'ways act as a shin' example- in all ways - to the expandin' population of our beautiful city of Athens Georgia.

Yo' grandmother, Miss Louisa Boulin – God rest her soul - neva forgot her station and certainly neva' let an opportunity pass durin' which she could exhibit her fine breedin' in its best light to those in the nearby vicinity – whateva situation might present itself – no sir, she was fo'eva a lady through an' through - as you will be my darlin' Esther – of that I have little doubt.

What's that darlin'? Yes, ah suppose you can go out to play for an hour or so. No, no, ah appreciate you are still only eight years old, Esther, but a girl – whateva her age may be - is neva too young to begin learnin' what sort of manners define a lady. Away you go, my darlin'... but don't let me catch you swingin' upside down from the rafters in the tobacco sheds.

You take care – hear?.

SUNRISE IN CHIRAN

Corporal Masahiro Nakamura stepped out into the dawn garden and inhaled deeply, filling his lungs with fresh mountain air. Was he ready?

He looked down at the paper still clutched in his right hand and reread the words, crafted by an artistic hand in traditional calligraphy.

> In blossom today, then scattered:
> Life is so like a delicate flower.
> How can one expect the fragrance
> To last forever?

Masahiro took a deep breath. The words of the poem had already burned themselves into his memory. Admiral Onishi had written those words for the men of the Special Attack Mission – the Pilots of the Divine Wind. Takijiro Onishi had written those words for him.

He recalled the afternoon last November when their base commander assembled his squadron and unveiled the latest plan from military headquarters. It had been decided, he explained, that the most efficient method of inflicting devastation upon enemies of the homeland would be to attack them from the sky. The forces had a number of aircraft that were expendable because of their age and condition. One person would fly each plane containing enough fuel for a one-way trip, destroy the given target and cripple the American fleet.

The General told his men to close their eyes and, when the question was put to them, to raise their hand in silence if they were willing to take part. Each pilot knew what was being asked of him. They had all been so excited and proud when they discovered that they had, to a man, become volunteers.

But now, as the time approached, it didn't seem such a clear cut decision. Masahiro shifted his left foot, pounding it up and down to regain the circulation in his leg. He shivered and his head was throbbing. Too much *sake*. It had been some party last night. In fact the last two days had been more or less one continuous party. The whole squadron had been feted and pampered ever since their arrival forty-eight hours ago. Considering they were at war, Masahiro was astonished at the treats that were pressed upon them. There was nothing in the way of pleasure that had been refused.

Women, any number, were on call to entertain in whichever manner any of the flyboys desired. And they were good-looking too, not just a bunch of hookers from the streets of Kagoshima, but high-class geishas from Gion. The music, singing and dancing was non-stop.

And the food – the food was plentiful, delicious and available at any time of the day or night. You just had to ask. And of course, there were oceans of beer, *sake*, whiskey and even opium for those who felt the need. It was obvious the government thought they were heroes and treated them accordingly. How would they view him now, wavering this way and that like a butterfly in the wind? The certainty of that day of decision seemed a long time ago. Were any of the others in the squadron now experiencing similar feelings?

Masahiro knew that his plane would be properly prepared and already waiting for him on the runway back at base. Private Maeda, the mechanic who was responsible for making it ready, had recently explained to him how he had not only tuned the engine to the best of his ability, he had also cleaned and polished every design detail on the inside of the cockpit as well. He felt it was his duty and privilege to turn each kamikaze plane into a coffin fit for a hero.

He adjusted the blanket around his shoulders as his eyes caught the first rays of a clear sunrise. Stars were fading, drawing away from the world and the sky was becoming brighter. The dawn light cast a web of gold over the countryside. Cumulus clouds floated high above the village. They reminded him of the paper boats he and his father had sailed in Lake Ikeda when he was a child. Across the valley he spied a flock of black-headed gulls swirled in the rising currents on their way to feed on the river. This was surely an auspicious morning. Weren't all the signs in place?

Masahiro recalled the guidance they'd all been given.

The pilot will approach his destination with great joy in his heart. He will fly under the sun and above the clouds. When he spots his target he will point the nose of his aircraft downwards, increase the throttle and fall out of the sky like a thousand, thousand cherry blossoms. He will be proud and with his final breath he will call out the names of those he holds dear. He will come to rest on the ocean bed where his body will spend eternity.

Masahiro picked up his leather stationary pad from the table near the door. He held it close to his face and inhaled; he could still smell its newness. It had been a gift from his uncle when he graduated from university last year. His degree in political science and economics meant little or nothing to him now. It seemed like another life.

His hosts, Fujii and Yuoko Tanaka, had treated him as a son during his stay in their home. Fujii-kun shared the same blood of the very samurai who had designed this garden more than six hundred years ago. He still tended it. Masahiro tried to picture the man who had created such a serene and beautiful place. He was a warrior, but not simply a warrior. He was also a scholar and a philosopher who, when he was not at war, desired only to be at one with nature. His garden reflected the landscape, with its conical mountains, perfectly manicured bonsai trees, rocks and moss-covered stone temples. Shouldn't this sight alone reinforce his determination to carry out his destiny? For the glory of his country and his Emperor?

He had waited till this morning to write to his family. The air was cool and fresh here in this quiet corner, and as he watched a tiny group of cinnamon sparrows quarrelling in the hedge, he collected his thoughts.

By now his father would be up and getting ready to go to work in his tiny office at the ferry terminal in Kagoshima. As a treat, he would sometimes take his young son on the fifteen-minute journey across the bay to Sakurajima where they would walk across the lava fields. They would use their umbrellas to protect their clothing from the black ash that rained down from the cone of the volcano.

His mother would be busy preparing a meal for the family. It would be nothing like the feasts he had devoured here in Chiran, for Masahiro knew that food had become a scarce commodity and women who weren't working for the war effort spent much of their day wandering through the markets in search of something to fill the shrinking bellies of their family.

Little sister, the baby, the spoiled one, Hiroko, with her laughing face, bounced into his mind. None of them could resist her antics and anything she asked for was given without resentment. He knew he was fortunate to have been born into such a family. The marriage of his parents had not been an arranged one. They had married for love.

He began to write.

"Dearest Father, Dearest Mother."

His pen moved across the paper. He hesitated. Perhaps if he wrote his way through this dilemma the right decision would become clear?

"Today is the most important day of my life. Today is the day I wish to thank you both, dearest ones, for giving me the gift of life. I love you very much and it is because of my love for you both and for my little sister, Hiroko that I have agreed to give this life to protect you, our country and our esteemed Emperor God.

Father, thank you for all the sacrifices you made to enable me to go to university. In different circumstances I would have been able to repay your generosity.

Mother, I do not wish to leave you anything of mine because I know you would look at it over the years and weep. That must not happen. You are my beloved mother and I will think of you when I am flying above the clouds before I die.

Hiroko-chan, thank you for the doll you sent me. It looks like you. I will take it with me in the cockpit as an amulet. It will help me think of you before I attack the enemy as I go to my death.

I have made plenty of money in the army, little sister, and I want you to have it so you can go to school and be educated.

Do not waste the money.

Use it wisely for education is a wonderful thing. And remember, Mother and Father will need your help in your new life together."

Masahiro stopped writing here for a moment as he pictured the sweet face of his sister once again. He shook his head, tried to dispel the thought. He remembered how, when she was learning to walk, she would dog his steps, pleading for him to wait for her. She was a pretty young girl now and would grow into a beautiful woman, of that he had no doubt. Could he bear not to see that? *Keep writing,* he told himself, perhaps it will all become clear.

> "I am happy and proud of what I am about to do. Do not weep for me but think of me with love. Come to see me at Yasukuni Jinja on my 22nd birthday where I am told the rice cakes are very large.
>
> I will be waiting to talk to you.
>
> Good-bye.
>
> Your loving son and brother,
> Corporal Masahiro Nakamura"

The young airman put the letter into an envelope embossed with the insignia of his squadron. He tried to imagine his family reading its contents.

He slipped into the bath and sat back for a few moments with his eyes closed. As he opened them again he could see the cherry trees that lined the street beyond the wall. They were in full bloom and the drooping branches were heavy with clusters of fresh, pink blossom. He could see the sun rising now behind the cherry trees and simultaneously he felt something almost physical rise upwards in his throat. His reaction to such exquisite natural beauty surprised and shocked him. He felt a great rush of tenderness, an almost overwhelming pride and responsibility for his homeland and its people, his family and their future. In that moment his soul was swept clean of any doubt. All concerns dissolved into nothingness. Rising from the water, Masahiro felt he had been reborn.

He paid special attention to the state of each article of his uniform as he dressed in front of the mirror in his bedroom. Everything today must be perfect. He leaned over, tucked the legs of his trousers into the tops of his boots as he pulled them on. Lastly, he shook out a brand new white silk scarf and wrapped it around his neck. He tied Hiroko's doll to his shoulder. It was feather light. He took one final look around the room. No, he decided, he would not need anything else.

Flying in a prescribed formation, known as 'the floating chrysanthemums', his squadron would be heading, in less than two hours, toward Okinawa and the American fleet. On the sortie as part of Kikusui No.6.

And he, too, would be airborne.

HAVING A BALL

Sharp pangs of regret began stabbing at my soul the second she answered the door. This was all wrong. I blinked but stood my ground, taking my cue from Joyce who was close beside me and who was also two whole years older than me. We both smiled as innocent a smile as we could muster. We tilted our heads, blinked our eyes in a flirty sort of way, and stared up at the fragile, sun-deprived face that hovered above us.

Miss McPherson wasn't much taller than me. She wore what looked like an artist's smock over her dress. It was covered with dabs of dried paint. The thought flashed through my mind that I would have been in serious bother at home if I had done that to one of my tops.

"What a lovely surprise, girls!" Her eyes flitted to the covered plate that Joyce was carefully balancing in her right hand. "Do come in."

Her soft voice was warm and when she said 'girls' it sounded like 'gir-r-rals'. In fact, it reminded me of the way Gillian Morrison's granny talked. She had come to Canada all the way from Scotland to live with the Morrison family after Gillian's grandpa had died. Of a heart attack, Gillian told me.

Miss McPherson pulled the door open wide and almost before we knew it, Joyce and I were stumbling over the threshold into her private world. I felt quite uncomfortable as Miss McPherson invited us to sit down. There were only two chairs in her room, so I sat near the wall on the edge of her bed. The pink candlewick bedspread felt lovely and fluffy against my bare legs. I sat stock still and could see that Miss McPherson was waiting for one of us to explain the purpose of our visit. All of a sudden the idea we cooked up earlier that afternoon lost its appeal. But now that we were here, what could we do but carry on with our misguided plan?

It all started at home when our phone rang just after lunch. It was Joyce asking if I would like to come over to play. My younger brother was moaning because he had to wash the dishes and complaining I wasn't quick enough at clearing the table. Mom shushed him and agreed that I could go as soon as I was finished my chores. I put on a spurt and swept the kitchen floor in record time.

"Don't be late for supper, Duchess!"

"I won't," I called over my shoulder as the screen door slammed and I raced down the back alley.

When I arrived at Joyce's place she was playing hopscotch alone on the street in front of the hotel. That surprised me because she's two years older than I am and even I hardly ever play that game anymore. I felt quite pleased that she had called me though, because when she and Linda are together, they act as though they don't know me. They giggle a lot and talk about stupid stuff like boys and cars.

When school starts up in September, they'll be going to high school. Linda was away for the weekend and I figured Joyce must be really missing her. I picked up a stone and joined in. We didn't play long, but I didn't mind because Joyce let me win.

"Let's go to watch the train come in and see if any travellers will be coming to stay at the hotel tonight." Joyce threw a scuffed old India rubber ball against the wall over and over again as she spoke. It didn't matter how high it bounced, she caught it every single time.

"Will you stop making that confounded noise this minute?" Her father's bald head popped out of his office window and cigar smoke was pouring out of his mouth as he yelled at Joyce. I turned my back because I thought I was going to burst out laughing. He looked like some kind of dragon monster out of the comics as he leaned over the sill. Joyce didn't say anything back. She just grabbed her ball and started to run across the street to the railway station.

"C'mon, Pokey Joe - last one to the platform's a rotten egg."

The only people who eventually stepped down from the train were Mr Gilbert, an old bachelor who kept chickens and lived in a ramshackle house on the edge of town, and Mr and Mrs Kraus whose family had given them a gift for their wedding anniversary of a trip back to the 'old country'. I had seen a photograph in the Wilkie Press of their party a few weeks back. So, it looked like there weren't any strangers coming to town today.

A game of catch seemed in order. Joyce and I sauntered back to the sidewalk in front of the hotel and threw her ball back and forth, back and forth, until we were too bored to do it anymore.

"I know what we can do." Joyce stuffed the ball into a pocket of her baseball jacket. "Let's ask Mom if we can go into the kitchen and make ourselves something to eat."

We found her mom sitting behind the reception desk. She was busy smoking a cigarette and looking at pictures in the latest copy of Life Magazine.

"What is it, sweetie?" her mom asked without taking her eyes off the page. I'm not sure she really paid attention when Joyce told her what we wanted to do. She just waved the hand that was holding her cigarette like she was shooing away a fly and drawled, "Go ahead. Just don't make a mess."

We ran to the kitchen with all its cold counters of stainless steel and all its equipment and talked about what we should make. I thought she meant a sandwich or something like that, but Joyce decided a chocolate cake would be best, so we got started. While it was baking we made up a bowl of lovely smooth vanilla icing. When we finished decorating the cake there was still quite a bit left over. Joyce claimed if we just sat and ate it we'd probably make ourselves sick.

That was when we came up with our *brilliant* idea. Well, it was her idea, really.

Joyce retrieved the ball from her jacket pocket and we set to work. First of all, we sliced a bit of the ball off the top with one of the very sharp knives we found in a drawer and turned it upside down so it would sit nicely on the counter. Then we made four cuts, each one from the top to the bottom of the ball. By the time we had finished with it, the ball looked roughly like a piece of plain chocolate cake. We took our time icing it. With the top and all four sides covered we were certain no one would know it wasn't the real thing.

"Let's put a cherry on the top."

"Okay." Joyce searched out a cherry and we

thought our creation looked perfectly wonderful sitting on a delicate bread and butter plate. We stood by the counter munching our own still warm slice of cake and congratulated ourselves on a job well done.

"What should we do with it?" I wanted to know. Joyce cocked her head and swallowed some cake before she picked up the pretty plate and asked "Do you know Miss McPherson?"

On our way upstairs Joyce told me a little bit about our victim. Quite a long time ago, before I started school, Miss McPherson was a teacher at McLurg Public School. She developed a 'case of the nerves' and now Joyce said she was an angry-phobic which meant that she didn't come out of her room anymore. She had lived in The Dew-drop Inn for years and sometimes when Joyce passed her room, she could hear the old lady walking around and talking to herself. She sounded quite scary to me.

Miss McPherson was still sitting with her hands settled in her lap waiting for one of us to speak. The plate sat on a flimsy TV table beside Joyce's chair.

"We've brought you something that we made this afternoon, Miss McPherson." Joyce removed the floral napkin from the pretend cake with a flourish. "This is for you."

When I saw how Miss McPherson's face lit up I lowered my eyes. I couldn't go on with this. It wasn't a joke anymore. As Miss McPherson picked up the ball and was about to bite into it, I jumped off the bed.

"It's a sponge!" My cheeks were burning. Joyce ignored me.

"Oh, that's one of my favourites." And to my dismay her smile broadened. Joyce shot me a warning look and started to giggle as the hand holding the cake was moving ever upwards.

"No, I mean it's a *sponge* - a real sponge!"

"Yes, dear, I understand – and lovely it looks too." Her hand paused near her mouth. She looked at me with a small frown. "Thank you very much – both of you."

My breath caught in my throat as she bit into the ball. When her jaw bounced open she made another valiant attempt to rip off a piece before she removed the 'cake' from her mouth. She pursed her lips and wriggled her jaw back and forth a couple of times to settle her dentures back into place before she looked at the two of us. I wish what happened next could be wiped from my memory; her extreme embarrassment, our everlasting shame. When we tried to explain what we had done and how we thought it would be such a joke, Miss McPherson inhaled and let out her breath in a deep, deep sigh. She kept the napkin and handed the plate back to Joyce.

"I think it would be best if you took your little 'joke' and left." She seemed even smaller now as she turned away from us and walked toward the window. We slunk from the room, closed the door as quietly as we could and walked down the corridor without speaking a word. I told Joyce I thought it was time for me to go home.

At suppertime I pushed the food around on my plate.

"Did you have something to eat at Joyce's?" Mom asked me.

"Yeah – I had cake."

"I'll bet you two girls had fun this afternoon, didn't you?"

I shrugged. What could I say?

"Yeah – we had a ball."

Having a Ball and Other Stories

BLACKCURRANTS

An old woman speaks :

I sit on this corner most days. In times gone by the ladies of the city would gather here to drink coffee and absinthe and to gossip. Sometimes I sell things in little pots – mushrooms from the forest, wild blueberries, cherries – depending on what I can collect. Other times I just sit…

 Most people don't know my name. Some call me 'babushka' – they say "Good morning, babushka" or "Good evening, babushka" and I smile and reply "Good day to you, kind sir, kind madam." Others pretend not to see me and pass by with averted eyes. I don't mind either way…

What I love is when the school children come up and speak to me, like they did this morning. They are shy, but so fresh, so innocent. They asked me where I live and why I come and sit on the corner near the Thirteen Teardrops. They didn't notice that I ignored the first question.

So, I told them – this is a beautiful place to sit, is it not? See the trees where the birds nest and sing… the sky today is bright and blue, and just now I can watch the workmen who are repairing the buildings and relaying the cobbles. Can you hear them singing the old songs while they prepare Riga for her 800th birthday? What a celebration that will be…

I went on too long this morning, I think, and the children soon became distracted. They said goodbye and ran on their way like a small group of chattering starlings.

When I lift my eyes to the left, over the trees, I can see the magnificent black tower of the Dome. I can't see too well any more, but if I tilt my head, just so, and narrow my lids, I can nearly make out the tiles on the roof. When the organ master is rehearsing, I position myself nearer the main doors where I can hear him.

Sometimes the music reminds me of a gentle wind that would rustle through the cornfields, in the old days, when the crops were dry and ready for harvesting. At other times, his playing sounds like a thunderstorm and I don't know if it is the ground that is shaking or just me.

I look over the square where I can see all kinds of people crossing the ancient cobbles, watching them dodge the barriers where the workmen are busy. Most of them walk with a purpose. Young, energetic, with well-cut suits and flowing coats that tell me they must be very important people with very important places to go and very important matters to discuss.

Oh yes, quite often I watch the serious young musicians choosing a spot nearby where they stand and play soulful music. People passing by sometimes drop coins into their cases and the musicians give a solemn nod of thanks. Their fingers are agile, not gnarled and stiff like mine, and they move over the instrument – flute, violin, or whichever – with light movements that make it appear each piece is being created there and then.

I once noticed a slight girl playing an old, battered violin with great tenderness. In front of her was a black dog that sat completely still, staring straight ahead. It held the handle of a small willow basket gently between its teeth. I was touched by what appeared to be such companionship between the two. Later that day I saw the same girl angrily kicking and beating the dog with the buckle of her belt. The dog cowered and trembled, but it didn't attempt to run away. I realised that it wasn't love, but rather fear, that had kept the dog so still.

Thanks be to God, I've sold the last of my blackcurrants, and look at that – I've got two lats. Should be enough for a hot meal tonight - potatoes and perhaps some meat. And a warm bed…if I'm not too late to get a place at the hostel.

These old legs swell up when I've been sitting too long, but it shouldn't take more than half an hour to walk through the Old Town and past Freedom Statue. Just down from the hostel there's a small café, over the bridge near the market, where Vadim, the chef, works. Vadim is a good boy. Sometimes he gives me extra bread and bits of meat that are easy to chew.

He was raised on the same collective farm where I worked before we got our freedom. When the farm was divided up and Vadim's father was sent away with one emaciated cow and a starving pig, Vadim realised he had no future in the country.

I myself came away with twenty lats because I couldn't work anymore. Not much use to anyone in our brave new world - a working life and years of heavy toil with nothing to show for it but twenty lats and this creaky old body. You have to smile…

I know I'm finished, but the thought of young Vadim cheers me. He works hard and over these last nine years of independence I can see our country's future through his success. We left our home on the farm and travelled into the city on the same day. Neither of us knew how we'd fare.

Now he has a home and a young family. Sometimes he invites me to visit and his wife gives me tea and cake. His children call me Auntie and ask me to tell them stories about the old days. I tell them of my childhood in the days before the communists came to free us from the Nazis, but forgot to leave. That's my little joke.

I was born between the wars in the few years of my country's freedom and now I am happy in the knowledge that I will die in a country that is free once more. In my heart I was always Latvian first and communist second.

And now here I am, an old woman who freely chooses to sit and watch and listen. I am watching and waiting.

Just waiting…

THE CLEARING

The stench of decay was overpowering. June pulled her rubber gloves over the cuffs of her boiler suit and looked at the disgusting mess surrounding her.

"Another day, another dollar," she muttered into her mask.

"What was that?" called a muffled voice from the small kitchen area.

"It doesn't matter,"

Her sharp grey eyes checked out the window frame and saw to her great relief that it wasn't painted shut. She skirted around the shabby sofa and unscrewed its stiff lock before throwing the sash as high as it would go. She took a deep breath of fresh air and turned to survey the room. The day was promising to be another hot one and that certainly wasn't helpful when there was a job like this to be done.

June arrived at the depot early today so she could organise her heavy duty equipment. After yesterday evening's instructions she knew that this clearing was going to be an unpleasant one.

She usually approached the job with a sense of respect for the late resident. She always felt that when someone died alone and unnoticed, the least she should do is to leave her own prejudices and emotions at the front door. Their department was never given many details about the place they were going before they arrived and she appreciated that it wasn't really any of their business either. All June knew about this case was that it was a middle-aged white male who was a sudden death (a heart attack, according to the coroner's report) and who wasn't discovered until his neighbour across the hall called the council to report a terrible smell in the corridor. Having investigated all possible sources, his flat was finally broken into and the body found. The police reckoned he had been dead for about a week and a half. At this time of the year that was bad news.

She and Sheila were on the job by nine o'clock. The van driver would be back by mid-afternoon to collect the contents. It shouldn't take them any longer than that to clear a one bedroom flat.

"God, this guy lived like a pig!" Sheila put her head around the door. "C'mere and have a look."

"I don't have to leave the sitting room to see that."

They took turnabout on the job and she was grateful that Sheila had picked the short straw today and had to clear the bathroom and bedroom while she was to see to the rest. June knelt down and began to pick up the shards of what looked to be a beer glass from the floor near the gas fire. She wrapped the pieces up carefully in the stained and greasy blanket that she grabbed off the sofa and tossed the whole lot into the first of many heavy black bags she knew she would be using that day. Their squad was trained to take special care on the job with anything they touched in case of injury or possible infection. She felt certain that the squalor in this place was a fine breeding ground for plenty of unsociable bacteria.

She went over to a small chest under the window and nearly pulled it over when she attempted to open the top drawer. It was sticky and the unit was unstable. She found an old benefits book and an out-of-date passport along with the usual pencil stubs, pieces of string, old buttons and dust. June glanced at the passport and saw that the only stamps on its pages were from Shiphol Airport and the latest one was dated about five years ago. She flipped over to the picture and saw an unremarkable face. A plain, fifty-something man with light coloured hair and not too much of that. The blue eyes behind over-sized specs looked self-consciously back at her.

"Well, Mr. McDougall, that was you in your prime, was it?"

She quickly emptied the contents of each drawer and moved on to a pile of magazines behind the brown armchair. She was about to scoop the whole lot into the bag when she noticed the cover of the one on top. Its title looked foreign. June was caught off guard when she realised that they were all pornographic. She turned a few pages and stared in disbelieving amazement. It was definitely hard core and every page was full of people in obscene poses or doing sickening things not only with each other but also with animals and in particular with children. She thought she had seen almost everything in this job by now but this garbage really took the biscuit. What was the matter with the man, she wondered as she grabbed the pile and chucked it into a separate bag. This would definitely have to be passed on to the vice department. And now it wasn't only the smell of the flat that made her stomach churn.

The magazines were the first of a number of finds that indicated the way McDougall (she couldn't think of him as Mr. anymore) had obviously lived his life.

If they had time, once in awhile the two women made a detective game out of their work, using items they found as clues to build up a fantasy picture of the departed.

Besides the porn, when Sheila started in the bedroom, she found an assortment of sex toys, an old polaroid camera and a battered sample case full of women's lingerie that looked like it had been in the wardrobe for quite a while. The contents were certainly no longer pristine and some of it was very exotic. All the pieces looked as though they had been well fingered over the years. There was a partially used pad of order forms yellowing in a dresser drawer that had the logo of a long defunct company at the top. June tried not to be judgmental but that case gave her the creeps and she couldn't help thinking that he must have been *some kind* of salesman. And she thought it a bit odd that after all the 'hard stuff' she found in the lounge, she should then come across a stash of old children's comic books hidden under his mattress. It didn't make a lot of sense to her.

In the kitchen there was very little in the way of food, thank goodness. She always hated confrontations with rodents. The poor blighters would have starved to death in this place anyway, she thought. There was an opened can of Guinness on the draining board and six more with reduced labels on them in the cupboard next to a bottle of cheap rum that hadn't yet been opened and a couple of cans of Heinz Tomato soup. A Safeway bag full of empties was also lying on the floor next to the bathroom. He obviously liked his booze. There was little else in the flat of any interest. Few papers and no letters. McDougall appeared to have no family or known relatives. A loner by the looks of it.

They finished the job much earlier than they thought they would. It gave them a rare chance to sit in the sun on the steps outside the building and enjoy the tea that was left in their flask.

When the van returned there were two strong guys along with the driver and it only took them twenty minutes to pack up the man's life. While she was carrying a dusty mirror in a heavy frame down the stairs, June noticed a piece of paper fall from the back of it. She rested the mirror on the bottom step and leaned over to pick it up. She felt as though she had been punched in the solar plexus when she realized what she was seeing.

"Sheila – look at this!"

With shaking hands, June passed the paper to her friend who took one look and collapsed onto the steps.

"Oh no, oh no…" She stared as tears rolled down her cheeks.

It was a tattered photograph of a teenage girl with long auburn hair. She was scantily clad and posing provocatively. Wearing a long translucent veil draped artistically over her youthful body, she stared directly into the camera. June recognised McDougall's bedroom and the lingerie. There was no mistaking the subject.

"In school we all thought she was so beautiful. Remember how she always wanted to be an actress?"

Sheila choked as she wiped the back of her hands across her eyes.

"Everyone used to tell her that she looked just like Rita Hayworth. I couldn't believe that she'd never come back."

June looked again and saw something scrawled across the bottom. She held it up to the daylight and could just make out the faded writing -

To Darling Uncle Sandy,
from his Angel XXX

HERO

Colin's new shoes were so shiny he could practically see his own reflection in them. And if he could have done he would have been proud of his wide smile and very neat hair. His mum had taken him to an actual grown-up barber yesterday. Usually she trimmed his hair at home with her special scissors. He always has to sit perfectly still on the stool whenever she has those scissors in her hand.

"Colin, you sit perfectly still now," she would say. "Don't you move – a hair!"

She wrinkles her nose and then they both giggle before she wheels her chair around behind him and begins cutting. It's one of their secret jokes.

Yesterday morning he didn't even have to be reminded to sit still. When he climbed onto the high black chair he knew just how to behave. Mum said that the barber even commented on how well he had done for his first time there. Colin was quite proud too as he watched the barber's reflection in the massive mirror.

When they left the barbershop Colin stood for a moment and watched the red and white pole turning above the door. Mum said it was electric and that was why the colours looked like they would twist right off and drop on the pavement in a puddle by his feet. It was just an 'opi-collusion' his mum told him. The colours wouldn't really slide off. He could have watched that pole turning for a long time but they had to go and buy Colin 'something smart to wear for tomorrow' his mum said.

And now here it was tomorrow and here he was sitting on a wooden chair that shuggled a little bit if he rocked back and forth. He knew that would be bad manners to shuggle but he thought no one would notice if he just did it gently. It was quite lonely sitting up here on his own while his mum and everyone else was sitting down there looking at the man who was standing with his back to Colin and throwing his hands all over the place.

Colin knew the man was called the provost and his mum told him that the provost is probably the most important person in this whole town. Colin was impressed when he learned that fact and last night he had a strange dream about a giant with a huge fork who ate telephone wires like they were spaghetti and picked his teeth with the poles when he had finished. The giant claimed he was the provost. But this man doesn't look anything like Colin's giant.

It was strange that when Colin slept he could hear sounds and noises. It didn't make sense that when morning came and he opened his eyes, all about him was silent again. He liked hearing sounds.

The provost turned toward Colin. He was holding a dark blue box in his hands. His cheeks were red and he was gazing straight at Colin. Colin suddenly felt quite hot in his shirt and tie. He looked past the provost and saw his mum. He could see that everyone was clapping and right in the front row his mum was mouthing instructions to him. She had told him before they left the house in the special taxi that he would be fine and that if he kept watching her she would tell him what he should do.

"Come on, Colin – stand up son."

Colin stood up. The provost was beckoning to him so he took a couple of steps toward the man. He smiled and as the provost smiled back, he reached out and put his hand on Colin's shoulder. They stood side by side as the audience began clapping again. At the back of the room people with huge cameras began taking pictures and there was even a woman with a camera on a tripod that was aimed right at Colin.

Colin's mum told him that he was receiving a very special award for bravery. He had been 'commended' his mum told him. He couldn't quite make sense of it though.

Even now as he remembered the incident, he felt confused. They had gone out for a walk in the park that day last summer. In the afternoon. He had been pushing his mum's chair and they had stopped for a little rest. He knows he was the only one who saw what happened. As he sat on the grass beside her, he noticed his mum's face take on a strange look. He saw her manoeuvre her chair near the edge of the path where there was a pram parked. There was a little baby in the pram. So he was surprised when he watched her look all around and then give the pram a shove. It began rolling into the canal. He didn't know why she had done it and he knew he had to get the baby out of the water. He thought what his mum had done was wrong. But he knew she must have had an explanation. The baby's mum and dad rushed over from the picnic table by the hedge. Colin lifted the baby out of the pram before it sank in the mud. The daddy took the dripping baby into his arms and they both cried as they thanked Colin over and over again. Colin's mum had smiled at him too and wrinkled her nose.

They had had to go to the police station for his mum to fill in an accident report. When they got home later that day, she cuddled and hugged him. She told him that since Colin's daddy went away, she felt so sad at times that she did things even she didn't understand. But she wasn't going to admit that to anyone else. Colin stared at her as he sat cross-legged on the floor and picked at his thumbnail.

"This is our little secret, isn't it, son," his mum signed to him.

Colin smiled and nodded.

THE PRODIGAL

A three character monologue

Mr. McFadden –

Late at night the sound of the doorbell always makes me jump. Considering the number of years I've lived in this manse it seems strange that it still startles me. The elders tell me I shouldn't answer it when I'm alone in the house, but I can't just ignore it – after all, I would hate to think there was a poor soul on the other side of that door who was in need of spiritual solace and I failed him by refusing to open it…

When I turned the key and pulled open the door, I was stunned – it was Alistair looking much worse than I had ever seen him. Taffy was bouncing around our feet, jumping up and down like a thing possessed. It had been a long time since he had seen the boy, but he recognised him immediately.

"Get down, Taffy," I growled at him "Get down."

I don't like raising my voice, but when he's excited his hearing seems to go.

"Alistair, come away in, lad," I said to the sad scrap of humanity standing in the doorway.

When he stepped into the hall, I saw just how thin and scrawny he had become. I had learned from his previous visits not to go on about how he was looking and I knew reaching out to him would be a mistake. It was hard to work against my natural instinct.

"I need some money," he said. Not explaining or asking, just saying outright.

"Alistair," I said, "I've told you before, I never keep cash in the house."

It always makes me smile when I hear of minister's houses being burgled or ransacked – obviously, the sort of people who do that don't know much about the church. There's certainly nothing of any great value in this house.

"Follow me into the kitchen," I said. "I can probably find something in there to fill up that hollow leg."

I know when he was growing up his mum always used to say "I honestly think Alistair must have a hollow leg – the amount of food he packs away." But that was a long time ago now. I'm just happy she never saw him looking like this.

I found some bacon and noticed that it was past its sell by date, but it still smelled alright even if it was looking a little bit green around the edges. I tossed it in the pan along with a couple of large eggs from the carton a farmer left me after the service this morning. It's one of the perks. I tried to make him feel comfortable and didn't ask too many questions. He looked worn out, but even so, his eyes were bright and shiny, just like an angel's. He had been such a good-looking lad when he was growing up.

"Smells good, doesn't it?" I said.

"Don't know what it is about bacon and eggs that

make you feel like eating even if you're not hungry – here, get yourself around this," I said and pushed the plate across the table.

Old Taffy had settled back down and was sitting in his basket by the cooker staring at Alistair in mute adoration.

It happened so fast I can't quite get it straight in my head. One minute he was sitting in the chair and the next he was hurtling toward me, with a face ugly and twisted.

"You'll never change, will you, you stupid old bastard?"

I felt a blow to the side of my head and Catherine Wheels danced in front of my eyes as I fell back against the fridge. He kept screaming all kinds of obscenities as his fists pummelled my body. I was stunned at his strength. Taffy thought it was a game at first and tried to join in but Alistair kicked the poor old fellow and I remember thinking, "Please God, stop him before he goes too far…Please, Gentle Jesus, help me…"

When I came to, I was still on the floor by the fridge and I felt stiff and cold. I pulled myself to my feet with the help of a chair and stumbled over to the sink where I threw up everything I'd eaten today. Poor old Taff had dragged himself back into his basket and was looking very sorry for himself. "Hey, little fellow, you didn't deserve that," I told him. He wagged his tail a couple of times but didn't come to me. I knew Alistair was gone. The food was cold and congealed on the plate.

I've managed to get myself up the stairs now to survey the damage in the bathroom mirror and heaven save us, what a mess I look. I suppose when I clean myself up I'll be able to hide most of the bruising –

except what looks like is going to be a real old-fashioned 'shiner' over my left eye. No one must ever know what happened here tonight. I'll tell anyone who asks that I tripped over Taffy in the kitchen and fell onto the cooker. They'll believe me - ministers don't tell lies. God help me…

Alistair –

As I rang the doorbell I knew the old bastard would answer it even though it was past time for social calls. He can't resist it. I was really beginning to hurt… I needed a hit and fast. He still looked the same as ever, rubbing his hands when he saw me, like a god-damned Uriah Heep. And that stupid dog jumping around our feet really pissed me off. It looked so happy I just wanted to give it a kicking. He took me into the kitchen and was whittering on like an old woman about feeding me. The thought of food made me feel sick. It's not food I need. As usual he didn't listen to me. While he was cooking I noticed that old print still hung in the same old place – the one of Jesus knocking at the door with no handle. It fascinated me when I first noticed it.

He made a bad mistake when he gave me the bacon and eggs.

"Alistair," he said in that dry, preachy voice he always uses, "are you not going to give thanks?"

It's something about that voice – I lost it completely and everything inside my head melted…

"You stupid old bastard, you fucking old prick," I could hear myself screaming.

I kept hitting him and screeching the things that I knew he would most hate to hear. Then Taffy came running at us, so I gave him the toe of my boot as hard as I could. I actually lifted him into the air – that shut him up. The old man didn't move a hand to protect himself while I raged over him. His lips were moving – probably praying for sweet release to his dead god. He still keeps a little cash in that old tea caddy, so I took it and ran. I'm on fire, but as soon as I'm fixed up I'll check on the house and see if he called the cops. I dare him to.

Mrs. Morrison –

It was a real shock when I arrived at the manse this morning to find the minister looking like he had been through the wars. I should have known all was not well when Taffy didn't even bother to get out of his basket to greet me when I let myself in through the back door. I've always been afraid something like this would happen because he insists on letting everybody who comes to his door into the place. He's too kind and trusting. When I'm working around in the kitchen he often brings shifty looking people through and "Mrs. Morrison," he'll say, "could I ask you to make a sandwich and a cup of tea? We have a visitor." Just as though it was some high mucky-muck instead of a smelly old free-loader looking for a handout. It looked to me as though his luck had finally run out. I knew it was just a matter of time…

"Mr. McFadden, who's done this to you? Shall I call the police?"

"Oh, good morning, Mrs. Morrison," he said. "No, don't call the police."

"How long have you been sitting in that chair?"

It was shocking to see him in such a state.

"All night, I suppose," he said, quite quietly. "I must have fallen asleep after the accident."

"Accident?" I said. "What accident?"

"It's all rather silly, really," he said, but when he tried to smile, he winced.

"What is?" I said. "What's happened here?"

He told me this story of how he decided to make

himself a plate of eggs and bacon last night and how he tripped over Taffy and hit his head against the corner of the cooker. I can hardly believe that a fall could do so much damage. As he was telling me about it, something was niggling in the back of my mind. I couldn't think he'd lie, after all he is a minister, but I just got the feeling he was covering something up. You never know these days. Anyway, I decided that what he needed was a cup of strong hot tea, but I saw there was no milk in the jug. I felt in the tea caddy for some change to get a pinta from the shop across the road. Empty. Strange, I thought. Never mind. I brought my purse with me, so I'll just run and get it now. As I crossed the road I thought I saw Alistair standing by the post box but a van blocked him from view and when I looked again he wasn't there. I must have been mistaken.

I think of them, Mr. McFadden and Alistair when I hear the old Bible story of the prodigal son, it's just so sad.

THE POWER

Growing up as an only child isn't all bad. In fact some people quite like it. I didn't like being by myself. Sometimes I would look out our front room windows to the family of eight who lived across the street and it seemed they were always playing, chasing and fighting with each other. I only had my cat. But I had also created a whole world of people and places that kept me company for hours when I was alone.

My father was a mortician and his funeral home was at the rear of our back yard. Whenever other kids came over to play it wasn't long before they'd starting acting all spooky and asking me questions about dead people.

"What's it like sleeping with a corpse in your garden?"

"Is it true that your dad stuffs their bodies with leaves?"

"I heard he cuts them open to drain their blood. Is that right?"

Some of the things they asked were just too ridiculous. However, it did give me a certain air of mystery. I knew exactly what my father did in his profession, but I wasn't about to share that knowledge.

I decided I was different than the rest of them in

more ways than one. For one thing, within my own world I had convinced myself that I had the power to bring people back to life. I never told anyone about this remarkable gift because I knew it was so special that I couldn't use it at random. But when I heard that our school janitor had keeled over with a heart attack, I knew my time had come.

My father had finished his preparations in the mortuary and old Mr. Hermann was laying at peace in the casket chosen for him by his widow. I went to pay a visit. Dad was with the family making the funeral arrangements in the front room and all I could think of was how happy everyone would be when Mr. Hermann came through the door of their pretty white house on Second Street. I wove my way past all the caskets on display in the showroom and slipped into the family room next door where Mr. Hermann lay for viewing. I stood looking him. He looked like he was sleeping. The only thing that was different was that he was wearing his suit instead of the pyjamas he had arrived in and he had a set of shiny black rosary beads wound around his stiff, white fingers.

This was my moment, the reason I was put on this earth. I began to concentrate on summoning up my mighty power. And I began to stare. I could feel all my energy streaming out of my eyes and into the mortal remains of Mr. Hermann. I stared and stared at that waxen corpse until I began to feel as though my feet were leaving the floor. It wouldn't be long now, I told myself, before he would be sitting up in that casket and thanking me in his broken English.

I had not a doubt my powers were starting to get through to him. I was almost certain that his huge chest was beginning to move in and out. His lungs were probably filling up with air right at that moment. I switched my gaze to his eyelids. Was that a little flutter I detected? I couldn't be sure, so I kept staring as long as I could without blinking. He must nearly be back. He wouldn't be teasing me, would he? Pretending my powers weren't working on him? That would be just like him.

Slowly I reached up and opened his right eye. It was flat and dull like the jackfish my dad would often bring home after a day's fishing at the lake. I began to have doubts. I couldn't believe my powers weren't working. What was happening? Was I using them on the wrong person? Fate couldn't be this cruel, could it? As I was puzzling over this dilemma I was trying my utmost to get Mr. Hermann's eye to shut again. After all, my dad was a perfectionist and a corpse with one staring eye would not be overlooked.

I began to panic and didn't even want to think about what would happen if he found out I had tampered with his handiwork. It had taken my mom long enough to convince him that I would be responsible enough to own a cat, for heaven's sake. I practically had to swear in blood that I would never let it wander into the mortuary because everyone knew that cats ate dead things. And if it ever got to one of his bodies that would be the end of his business. And now what I had done might be the end of his business.

My dad was a member of the Chamber of Commerce and a part-time volunteer fireman. He coached the local hockey team and everyone in town respected him. It would be the end of his reputation. My heart began pounding and my breath came in short, ragged gasps as I pictured the consequences of my actions. Tears filled my eyes and my hand shook as I tried once more to get that eyelid back in place, but I just couldn't do it. I ran up the sidewalk and in through the back door.

Mom was in the kitchen getting dinner ready.

"Hi dearie, what're you up to this morning?"

I could hear Dad's gentle voice in the other room, still talking to the family.

"Mom," I said, "could you spare a minute and come out to the funeral home with me?"

She stopped setting the table.

"What for?"

"I've done something awful."

Mom tripped along the sidewalk behind me as I told her about Mr. Hermann's eye and how sorry I was for messing him up. Of course, she knew what to do and had put the matter right within seconds.

"What did you think you were doing?"

"I just had to make sure he was truly dead, Mom."

I felt my face burning. I couldn't tell her the whole story; I knew she would never understand.

That night as I lay in bed watching the lights of passing cars race around my bedroom walls, I had some very serious thinking to do. Either I had used my secret power on the wrong person, or, unbelievably, I had never had the power in the first place. If that was so, then I still hadn't discovered why I had been born, because I knew, without a doubt, that there was a purpose for me being here.

I just had to find it.

MISSIONARY

The young man glanced at his reflection in the long mirror and adjusted his collar as he strode across the polished floor towards the door. His fingers traced the intricate carving on its dark surface before he gently knocked and waited for permission to enter.

"Come," said the frail voice of authority from the other side.

The door swung open on well-oiled hinges and he saw his bishop standing by the window observing Gabriel, the ancient gardener, deadheading roses in a nearby flowerbed.

"Good of you to come, Father."

He stood and watched the older man turn and make his way over to the desk.

"Please, sit down. I trust your journey into town was uneventful."

"Yes, thank you, Excellency. No punctures and the roads were very quiet."

The priest moved with easy grace as he settled his tall frame onto the brightly upholstered chair nearest the desk.

At that point the secretary entered the room. He had learned the habits of his superior well over the years, and was carrying a wooden tray of refreshments. He poured both men a cup of tea before retiring to his small side office where he would continue to sort the late post.

The bishop was not a man who indulged in meaningless chat. His time was valuable, especially since the heart attack last year when the doctor warned him that, if he didn't ease up on his workload, the next one would be fatal. He continued to fill each waking hour working for the betterment, not only of the people of his diocese, but also of his country, to the greater glory and honour of God. The priest knew that he had not been looking forward to this meeting.

"My son," he began, as he sat down heavily in his chair, "I have watched you growing in faith and humanity since the time you came to me and asked to be considered as a candidate for the priesthood."

His long fingers clasped the simple cross on his chest.

"Since your ordination five years ago, your God-given gifts have shown you to be well suited to the vocation you were willing to acknowledge. From the beginning, I had high hopes for the contribution you would make to the Church during your lifetime."

He paused and they both sipped their tea as the young man waited for him to go on.

"Only I *had* hoped that that contribution would be here in this diocese and not in a country on the other side of the world."

He tilted his head and again was quiet for a moment.

"I have seriously considered your request to work in the missions and have decided, after some consultation and much prayer that you should be allowed to follow this path. There are few ordained men of God working for the salvation of souls in the country to which you feel drawn and there will be much work for you when you get there."

The young priest sat on the edge of his chair hoping that he wouldn't embarrass himself in the presence of this great man. His heart was beating rapidly and his teacup began to tremble on its saucer. He placed it on the small table to the right of his chair and in the same movement fell to his knees in front of the bishop.

"Oh thank you, thank you Excellency!"

He felt he could breathe again. He leaned over to kiss the ruby ring of office. Recovering his composure almost at once, he jumped up and stood grinning broadly while trying to keep from dancing around the room.

"Well, I didn't realise you were *quite* so anxious to leave us, Father."

The priest shuffled his feet like an errant altar boy and lowered his eyes.

"Forgive me, Excellency. Of course I shall miss…"

The bishop rose, stopping him in mid-apology, and suggested, as he walked him to the door, that they meet again in a fortnight to finalise the details of his departure. The interview was at an end. The young man left the building unaware of the eyes following him as he raced his battered black bicycle down the avenue and out of sight.

"May God go with you, my son."

The bishop turned from his window.

The two weeks flew by. All the plans were finalised. Flights, tickets and papers were in order. Now it was just a matter of tidying up odds and ends in the parish and awaiting the arrival in two days' time of the new priest from the south to take his place. The ladies of the parish had arranged a farewell party to be held on his last night for everyone to attend. Over the past days they had vied to outdo each other with their hospitality. He hoped they would continue their generosity to the new man. And the children with whom he had been so involved and had so loved surprised him by shyly presenting him with several small homemade gifts by which to remember them. Their actions touched him deeply. He promised that he would write to them when he was settled and tell them all about his new life in the faraway land.

His suitcase was packed days before the arrival of his replacement. He would be travelling light because he knew that his clothes were, in the main, unsuitable for the climate. The bishop had given him some money in order to purchase new clothing when he got there. It was felt by those in the know that that way he would be less likely to stand out in a crowd. Lord knew the colour of his skin and strange accent would set him apart anyway. Amongst other things, he had been given a book of national customs and etiquette to read and had studied its pages long into the night. Sometimes the things he read made him laugh and sometimes they puzzled him, but he never once questioned his own reason for wishing to live among his chosen people. Ever since he had learned about the dwindling numbers of priests in that country, he knew that was where his calling would take him.

On his last morning, the young man got up before dawn and left his room without waking the new occupant of the house. The party had been lively and late and he wished to be alone. He recited his matins and drank in the beautiful sunrise with eyes that felt as if they were seeing it for the first time. He would remember everything - the grass, the trees, the smells and the sounds - everything. The sky was clear and cloudless and each facet of nature seemed to tantalise his senses with a beauty of its own. He loved this land and he would miss it. He turned his back on the scenery and heard the car coming up the road to take him to the airport.

The plane was on time which was a relief because when he got to the departure area he was completely taken aback to find a huge crowd of people waiting to see him off. Evidently the party still hadn't finished. He hadn't been anticipating this and would really have preferred not to have such a fuss made on this occasion. His family and many of his relatives (some of them having travelled a considerable distance to be there), plus assorted folk from his parish formed a noisy, jostling circle around him as they wished him bon voyage. They were treating him like some kind of local hero and he found it difficult. There was lots of laughing, a few tears, and everyone was trying either to shake his hand or clap him on the back as they walked him to the gate. He was, however, curiously touched when a small group of children began to sing a song of farewell. Someone had taken the time to teach it to them and as he listened to their voices he was aware of an almost sinful pride in his people and his nation.

The time had come for a final word. Someone requested he give them his blessing before boarding the flight. He raised his hand, looked over the bowed heads of these kind and gentle people and wondered when or even if he would see again. After all, this foreign land, this Scotland is thousands of miles from his beloved Uganda.

THE GIFT

She turned the corner and glanced up. Lights from a flat on the sixteenth floor of the high-rise beckoned her. She smiled – Jerzy had waited up. She quickened her pace; almost home and her wallet was bulging with tips. Their first Scottish Hogmanay would be one to remember. The restaurant patrons tonight had been good-humoured, noisy and generous. After the last guests had left the premises the manager even encouraged the staff, as a treat, to choose some leftovers from the kitchen to take home. If she was careful, she mused, there would be no problem now paying next month's rent. She was sure they could even stretch to buying Jerzy a pair of boots in the sales. He didn't complain but it hurt her to watch him leave their home each morning to search for work in his shabby trainers.

As she passed a string of empty shops her attention was drawn by a slight movement in the doorway of the derelict tobacconist shop. A lean dog sat watching her from the shadows. Beside it a jumbled heap of dark blankets stirred. She saw a swollen hand reach out to stroke the animal. A muffled voice croaked, "Just you and me, boy, just you and me." The young woman stepped closer and without hesitation laid the parcel near the pair. The dog remained motionless. She didn't look back as she continued walking toward the light.

LIKE THE MOVIES

The party turned into the same old thing – everybody swilling beer, rock 'n' roll blaring from Carol's record player and couples drifting in and out of the living room looking for privacy to do some exploring. Jenny wasn't in the mood and decided the only way she could stand being there was by pretending she was in a scene from *Blackboard Jungle*. She slouched against the door frame with a cigarette in her hand and tried to look cool. Mike sidled up to her but he was no Russ Tamblyn. It wasn't going to work.

"I'd like to go home," she told him.

Charlie was less than impressed when the two of them came to find him. It had taken him long enough just to get Karen onto the sofa in the den and he didn't feel like driving back into town just yet. But Jenny could be stubborn and finally Charlie gave in. He grabbed another beer out of the crate and they were off.

Everyone said it was a tragedy – a real tragedy. But then Saturday night parties on the prairies always hold an element of danger. Sexual tension, six packs and fast cars when mixed can become a lethal brew. Four kids out on the town and now two of them laid out in a hell of a mess on enamel slabs in the back room of the funeral parlour. It *was* tragic. Really.

Straight roads and a clear moonlit night they said. It was difficult to piece the whole story together. Mike couldn't remember, Jenny wouldn't remember and the other two were dead. Karen was dead. Charlie had cheated on his fiancée and his indiscretion had cost him his life. Poor Charlie; but Karen, she didn't deserve to die.

When they arrived at the hospital the police told Jenny's parents that she and Mike had got off pretty lightly, all things considered. Just a couple of superficial cuts and, of course, there would be quite a bit of bruising; but, lucky her, she was alive. Not like Karen and Charlie, whose poor parents were at the registrar's office in the town hall right now handing over the death certificates that had been signed by Dr. Stevens, the local coroner.

****

For the first few days after the accident Jenny was stiff, sore and very quiet. In her room she was surprised when she first saw herself in the full-length mirror next to the door in her bedroom – partly because of the bruised and swollen reflection staring back at her and partly because, for a split second, she could have sworn she saw Karen standing beside her. Beautiful Karen with her coal-black hair and her long eyelashes that had all the boys buzzing round.

Karen and Jenny had been friends since before they started school. They had shared secrets and when they were eight they had cut their wrists and bound them together with a grass rope in a secret ceremony mimicking a complicated ritual they had seen in an Indian film at the Saturday matinee.

"Blood sisters to the end," they had solemnly vowed.

The girls began attending the Saturday movie on a regular basis and soon it became the highlight of their week. At two-fifteen they would meet at the entrance of the Roxy Theatre, rain or shine, and wait for Mrs. Webber to unlock the doors to paradise. As soon as they bought their tickets they would push up to the refreshment counter and do some quick arithmetic to see how much candy they could buy once they'd paid for their popcorn. Karen loved liquorice cigars while Jenny invariably went for spearmint jellies in the shape of evergreen trees. They would always negotiate a swap before the main feature began. Whatever they saw on the screen became the subject of their play for the next week.

When they saw *The Greatest Show on Earth* they stopped spending their allowance on candy so they could start saving to buy a circus when they were grown-ups. That same week they sat for long periods of time in Jenny's bedroom drawing up lists of calculations – how long it would take to have enough cash to buy an elephant, how many packets of sequins would they need for the trapeze artists' capes. And, of course, *they* would be those artists because, after all, they owned the circus. And so it carried on. Cowboys, pirates sailing the high seas (using the town's wooden water tanker that was parked in the vacant lot across the fence from Jenny's backyard as their ship), comedians or merry men, no world was beyond them in those magical times. They entertained each other, dancing like Fred and Ginger, walking like John Wayne or quoting lines from their favourite scenes –

"Alright Mr. De Mille, I'm ready for my close up."

Jenny and Karen remained close through the whole of high school and were looking forward to rooming together in the city while they attended teacher's college. They still went to the movies every week. Only now, more often as not, they went with boys who paid their way and then wanted to sit in the balcony where there were two rows of double seats and no surprises. On that Saturday they had gone to the early showing of *Blackboard Jungle* starring Russ Tamblyn. Karen had agreed to go with Charlie that night and Jenny was disgusted with them both because everybody knew that Charlie was engaged to Marcia. But Karen had said that no one would know they were together if Jenny and Mike went with them.

"C'mon, just for a laugh," Karen had smiled. "Charlie's so cute." She wrinkled her nose. Jenny agreed and when they left the theatre someone said that the party was at Carol's. So everyone piled into cars and pickups and headed out to the old Hanson place.

****

Autumn arrived and Jenny didn't go to college. In fact, she hadn't done much of anything since the accident. She rarely crossed the doorstep; couldn't see the point. Everyone in town said how well she was coping, but how would they know? They didn't seem to be able to understand that half of her died the night of the accident.

Mike came over once or twice before leaving for varsity. He promised to write. Other friends eventually stopped dropping by and life in town carried on just as if nothing had happened.

Jenny spent most of the time in her bedroom, stretched out on the bed and staring at the ceiling.

Occasionally her mother would come upstairs and stand in her doorway.

"Jenny, darling, I'm going to call Dr. Ash to see if he'll come over – just to talk to you."

"No don't, Mom – stop fussing, please. I'm fine."

"You know you're not, Jenny. Just listen to what he says. He won't force you into doing anything you don't want to do. Please, sweetheart, it's for your own good."

And so the conversation would begin again – her mother pleading, Jenny refusing all suggestions put to her. She didn't need a doctor's help. She needed to be alone.

Sometimes, in her bedroom, Jenny would talk out loud to Karen, reminding her of their private world – repeatedly going over the plans they had made together. She began to see her friend's shadow staring out at her more and more often when she looked in the mirror. Jenny knew she wasn't far away. She just wished her parents would stop going on at her.

One afternoon the sun came streaming across the floor and reflected off the mirror, it bathed the whole room in the most incredible light. Jenny turned her head on the pillow and slowly began to look around. She got off the bed and paced the room searching for some sign of Karen; she was here, that was certain. As she passed the dressing table and neared the door, Jenny stopped and listened. She heard the doorbell ring and the deep tones of Dr. Ash speaking to her father in the hall. In that second the decision was made, and quite deliberately Jenny stepped through the mirror and became eight years old once more.

.

Having a Ball and Other Stories

BROKEN

Agnes is in a darkening room with her son.

Just a second son, don't be anxious. I'll get down on my knees beside you. Don't be afraid. I've called the ambulance. They'll come as soon as they can. I'll not leave you.

Here, let me lift your leg off the sofa. Gently now. There you go. C'mon, I'll get my arms around you. Just like I used to do when you were little and woke up frightened of the dark. Remember? You'd call me and I'd come running to scare all the monsters away.

It was a shock to find you sprawled on the floor tonight when I got in from work. I wondered why the house was in darkness. You never liked the dark. And when I came into the sitting room and spied you on the floor, I thought to myself that this was it – this time you were dead. Are you still breathing, son? Please show me some sign of life. Anything. Anything to tell me you're still here. Don't leave me, James. My boy, my son. Stay with me.

James, I'm having trouble breathing, son. My chest feels like it's being crushed and my heart's racing. Like a wild animal trying to escape a trap. And what about you? Are you alive?

Dear God, you still haven't moved a muscle. Your poor forehead is covered in sweat, but you feel cold. Oh, James. I see all those angry puncture marks on your arm. Scoring, it's called, isn't it? See son, I'm learning. You've been so careful not to let me see these things. Never wearing tee shirts anymore. Always long sleeves and jeans. No bare feet. I know why. You didn't want to flaunt the evidence in front of me, did you, son?

You're soaking wet. Your spine is digging into my thighs. Let me turn you more on your side. There, that's better – I can lean against the sofa now. Oh my God, the needle is still stuck between your toes!

It's as though for the last three years I've been waiting for this. Ever since the night I was called into the hospital when you first overdosed. At least I thought it was the first time. I couldn't believe it. Thought it had to be some kind of mistake. I had trouble starting the car and when I did, I must've driven there like a maniac. I hardly remember getting to you.

The doctor told me then you were a heroin addict. He said he thought this time it was probably an accident. This time? When you finally woke up, you swore it was. Said it was the end of the line with you and drugs. Promised me it would never happen again - that you would get help. You were so scared that night. So was I. I sat next to your bed, watching your face and wondered where I'd gone wrong.

You were always such dear wee boy, James. When Daniel's liver finally gave up and killed him, I didn't know how we were going to live. We had nothing. I can still see you at his funeral when we stood together at the graveside and you reached for my hand and asked if you could have a kitten.

Remember how we celebrated with lime crush and ice cream when I found out I got the job at the supermarket? I thought then we'd be alright.

I haven't had a decent night's sleep since I brought you home from the hospital. Always worried that the day would come when something like this would happen. I've pictured it, anticipated it, had nightmares about it. Although I've tried not to let it happen – I know it's an addiction, but it's been the only constant on my mind. I still don't know if you're alive.

I'll rock you. Back and forth. Back and forth. Like I did when you were a little boy. That winter when you had whooping cough and couldn't breathe. Do you remember, James? We got through that together. We'll get through this. You'll be fine, son. Look at your dear face. So ravaged. Colourless skin stretched tight across your cheekbones. And that dark stubble on your chin.

Here, your forehead needs a wipe. I'll go gently, son. Across your face. Down your neck. Oh-h-h, James. I feel it. Your pulse. Your heart is beating. It's faint, but it's beating.

Having a Ball and Other Stories

UNDER THE LOCUST TREE

He didn't hear or even feel the bullet as it hit the back of his neck. All he knew was that one moment he was leaning on his makeshift crutch, calculating the best method of escape, and the next his gun was on the dirt floor and he was being dragged or carried from the burning barn to a nearby patch of grass underneath a locust tree.

Above his head he could see the petals of its white blossom, brilliant against the fresh blue of an early morning sky. The heat from the shimmering, orange flames and the billowing, black pine smoke from the tobacco shed reminded him of the inferno that had been Atlanta. Everything seemed to have an intensity that he hadn't experienced since his boyhood.

"Asia, Asia, c'mon down to the riverbank and we'll catch katydids and lightenin' bugs. We'll keep 'em in a jar and whoever catches the most will get out of doin' their evenin' chores."

He wanted to grab his older sister's hand as she stretched it out, but for some reason he couldn't move his arm. There was a commotion going on near the shed. A group of men dressed in cavalry uniform appeared to be removing a carbine from one of the soldiers and tying his hands together with rope. That's *strange*, he thought. He closed one eye and tried with the other one to focus onto the scene before him. What's going on here? he wondered. It seemed the officer in charge was reprimanding the fellow for acting contrary to orders.

"Sergeant Corbett, you heard what I said before the fires were lit! I wanted him taken alive!" The soldier raised his chin as if he had been struck in the chest but made no reply. Wilkes wondered if he was watching a play. He didn't recognise it. It certainly wasn't *Our American Cousin*. Of course it wasn't – that was…some time ago. Nothing seemed to be making any sense. Where was he? What had happened to him? How could one body feel so much pain? And why couldn't he move?

He could hear the lieutenant ordering some of the men to move him up onto the veranda of the house. The heat from the fire was intense. His whole body was trembling involuntarily now and as he was lifted the pain was excruciating. He lost consciousness for a few moments. He was back on the farm and his tearful mother was sitting beside him in the kitchen, begging him not to join the army. Father wasn't long dead and she was still dressed in her mourning clothes.

"Wilkes, I couldn't bear to lose another of my loved ones." He could feel her eyes boring into his soul. "Please, my darling, promise me!"

"Mother, you know how I feel about the Cause. So I want you to realise that I am doing this only for you. And now I promise."

His mother smiled, reached out and caressed his forehead. He could no longer see her. The bearers laid him down and tried to make him as comfortable as possible. But there wasn't a position that could ease what had become this exquisite torment. Never had he felt such sensations.

When he saw David, his loyal friend, standing a few yards away, tied now to the locust tree, looking tired and wretched in his filthy riding clothes, everything began to make sense. In his mind a sudden maelstrom spewed out the incredible events of the past sixteen days – the assassination, the escape, the chase and inevitably, the capture. He looked down at his hands and knew that he would be identified without doubt by those who knew him well. The initials JWB that he had tattooed in India ink between the forefinger and thumb of his left hand were a dead give-away. He had only been a child, desperate to impress, when he did that.

"I'll show you, Edwin!" he had said to his brother. "I'm no coward!"

His dark eyelashes trembled and drooped while the sounds around him disappeared. He was again in the anteroom of the state box at the theatre. He had slipped one of his visiting cards to the footman who was on guard outside and then simply walked through the door. It had been easier than he imagined. He was so well known to the staff that no one questioned his late arrival at the performance. The play was a very familiar one and he knew exactly how and when the audience would react to the dialogue. He quietly jammed the leg of a wooden music stand under the brass handle of the door and checked that it couldn't move. He slipped into the box, stroking the cold metal in his pocket. One of the guests, a small well-dressed woman, turned toward him and patted an empty chair inviting him to sit down. Her slender hand was encased in white lace. Their eyes locked for a single instant. At the same time Henry Hawk, who was now alone on the stage, delivered a line that made the audience roar with laughter. In that moment he had drawn his derringer, placed it behind the left ear of the unsuspecting Lincoln and, unhesitating, pulled the trigger. His victim's head fell forward and the deed was done.

Wilkes smiled inwardly; he knew that he had done something of utmost importance for the people of the Confederacy. Long live the South!

His adoring audiences thought there was nothing more to him than his good looks and his acting talent. But hadn't he known differently? And hadn't he proved it! He was not only one of America's greatest Shakespearean tragedians, he was now also a grand hero and the saviour of his nation. He had organised confusion and disarray in Washington by getting rid of the iniquitous man who wanted to change an entire way of life. A life that the people of the South had worked hard to create and one it would never willingly give up. And what's more, he had accomplished the feat without breaking his promise to his beloved mother. His place in history was assured, of that he was certain.

Oh God, his ankle felt fiery and the pain was now racing up his leg. He and David would have been able to travel so much faster if he hadn't landed so awkwardly on the stage after catching that damned spur in the bunting around the box as he leapt. Henry was completely distracted and the audience thought it was all part of the play when he appeared, yelling "Sic semper tyrannis!" He had felt the break immediately and his leg could scarcely support him as he ran past the stage crew. He had mounted his waiting horse at the back door and galloped off into the darkness.

His whole body was in purgatory and when he

thought the pain couldn't get worse, someone knelt beside him and attempted to lift his head. He could hear voices and recognised one of them as that of the lieutenant.

"Try to keep calm Mr. Booth, I sent for a doctor a while back and he's just arrived. He's going to try and help you."

Someone from behind cradled his head while a hand raised a glass of something – it smelled like whiskey – to his parched lips. The moisture felt good pouring into his mouth but his throat contracted when he tried to swallow. He choked as it ran down his chin and his body was thrown into spasm. He felt his eyes closing again and then his precious Lucy was kneeling next to him. Her gentle hands placed a cool cloth on his forehead and her fingers began to lightly stroke his cheek.

"You're here my sweet, sweet girl. You know we'll soon be married and then I won't ever have to leave you again. Lucy, you are …."

The sounds he made were garbled. His tongue felt thick and useless; it stuck to the roof of his mouth. He wasn't certain she understood what he was trying to say. She didn't reply but as she smiled her face began to distort and he saw his mother once again.

"Tell her. Tell her."

The doctor leaned over the agitated young man and put his ear close to his patient's swollen and cracked lips.

"What are you saying, son?"

He felt he was drifting away. He was weightless. He could hear buzzing near his ears. Was it Asia come back with the lightning bugs? The pain was receding.

"Tell Mother I did it for my country."

In a sudden moment of perfect clarity, Wilkes realized that he was about to die. His eyes flew open as his breath became more and more strangulated. He didn't have any strength left to fight...

A few minutes later the doctor reached for the man's pale hands and folded them across his chest. He straightened up slowly and stretched to relieve the crick in his lower back as he turned to speak to Lieutenant Doherty.

"He's gone, I'm afraid. There was really nothing I could have done for him."

"What did he say to you, Doc?"

The old man shrugged and shook his head.

"I couldn't make out a word. I'm sorry I can't say. It seemed to me they were just noises."

THE SEARCH

Jessie knew she hadn't lived here long. She was sure that if she had done she would know where everything was and wouldn't have to spend her days searching for her possessions. Surely the staff wouldn't be interested in anything that belonged to her. However, she had heard rumours. Putting such unpleasant thoughts aside she got to her feet. This recliner was so comfortable. It was genuine leather. She could tell by the smell. She thought it must be quite new but just *how* new was a mystery. She began twirling around on the spot with her hands clasped together on her chest. In a hoarse voice she chanted long remembered lines.

"Dear St. Anthony please come round,
something's lost that can't be found."

There weren't many places she could have put the library books. Heavens, she was just reading them this morning after breakfast. Wasn't she? Once more she shuffled through a pile of papers. No, definitely not there. She crossed to the chiffonier. She loved the way the old wood gleamed. When her name came to the top of the waiting list at Moorgate Lodge, it was a relief to be able to bring some of her own furniture with her. Selling the flat had been so final. However, the decision had been made and now there was no going back.

Jessie yanked at the top drawer which was getting harder to open, and reminded herself that she must do something about getting it seen to before it seized up altogether. After satisfying herself that the books weren't there, she looked through the other four drawers and came up empty-handed. So frustrating. It wouldn't hurt to look once more. She might have missed seeing them. Jessie pulled the top drawer open again. A battered purple shoebox caught her eye. She grabbed the box and again whispered her prayer to St. Anthony as she removed the top. No, nothing. Just old letters and photographs that she had collected over the years.

She lowered herself into the recliner, held the box on her lap and began sorting through the contents. There she found one picture that she really loved of her and Douglas standing with Smuts when he was just a puppy before the girls were born. It was taken on the hill above the farm and you could see all the way down to the river. The whole time Douglas was overseas she had kept that photo at the side of her bed. Through the years he had worked heart and soul to provide for his family. At least until the organophosphates poisoned him and he was no longer fit to work.

Jessie shook her head as she remembered the day of the farm sale. Douglas didn't last long after that. Thank heavens the girls were married by then with families of their own. She smiled and sometimes even chuckled out loud. The box Brownie pictures and collections of well-thumbed letters from Douglas and the rest of the family brought to mind many cherished memories. When she had had enough reminiscing, Jessie decided it was time for a cup of tea.

She struggled to her feet, replaced the box in the bottom drawer of the chiffonier and stepped into her kitchenette. She laid a tray with a freshly ironed tea cloth (she was very particular about doing things properly) and a plate of chocolate gingers while she waited for the kettle to boil. When everything was set, Jessie took off her reading glasses, opened the fridge door and placed them next to the pile of library books on the second shelf. She brought out her fragile Lalique milk jug and put it on the tray before settling into her recliner to enjoy her afternoon cuppa.

Having a Ball and Other Stories

THE DINERS

They walked slowly to their usual table in the garden of The Woodman. After she was seated, he perused the menu and ordered the same thing they had eaten last Sunday. She sat close-mouthed next to him. Her nearness stirred him; feelings he thought he had buried made him ache. Inhaling her perfume as the waiter appeared, he smiled as if being caught in an illicit act and blushed as he ordered two large glasses of crisp rosé. It had always been their favourite. Only one glass a week now - for him, sometimes two. Never blinking, she stared toward the trees across the terrace. Wondering what had caught her eye, he followed her gaze and saw nothing but leaves on the turn. The food arrived at their table the same time as the wine. He raised his glass to her before cutting the beef in delicate pieces. Then he lifted her right hand, curled her fingers around the handle of the fork and hoped she would know what to do with it today.

The End

.

Having a Ball and Other Stories

AFTERWORD

Cowboy Days and Sunrise in Chiran have previously appeared in Markings.

Having a Ball and Other Stories

ABOUT THE AUTHOR

Lynn Otty grew up running wild on the Canadian prairies before settling down with her husband, family and pets in Southwest Scotland. She writes poetry and short stories, taking inspiration from many different sources. She is keen on foreign travel, having adventures and observing people, wildlife and nature.

Lynn has published a book of poetry entitled Window Dreaming. This is the first collection of her short stories.

Having a Ball and Other Stories

ACKNOWLEDGEMENTS

I would like to thank my editor Alison Williams for all her help in getting this collection ready. And thanks, too, to Mary Smith for giving me the encouragement to just do it; Jon Gibbs-Smith for his problem solving abilities and help in the unseen work of formatting and setting the whole thing out; and, Melissa Priddy for her delicious cover design. Thanks all.

30434404R00061

Printed in Poland
by Amazon Fulfillment
Poland Sp. z o.o., Wrocław